CREATIVE
EDUCATION

young
romance
books

For always

by Eve Bunting

illustrated by Robert Gadbois

CREATIVE EDUCATION

Published by Creative Educational Society, Inc., 123 South Broad Street,
Mankato, Minnesota 56001.
Library of Congress Cataloging in Publication Data
Bunting, Anne Eve.
For always.
SUMMARY: A teenager's trip with the skateboard team brings her to the
realization that teenage love does not necessarily have to last forever.
(1. Skateboarding — Fiction) I. Title.
PZ7.B91527Fo (Fic) 77-13085
ISBN 0-87191-636-3

Shelby heard her name called, and there was excitement, a sort of triumph that she'd made it. Ding Dong and the whole Wayne Skateboard Committee thought she was good enough.

She held tightly to Brian's hand and thought, please let him make the tour too. It'll be perfect if he does. If he doesn't. . .

The last two guys' names were called. And neither one of them was Brian's.

He turned to face her, and somehow it seemed that they were alone, even in the middle of all the hub-bub around them. Maybe that was why he kissed her. They normally didn't go in for kissing in front of a bunch of people.

"Hey, Shelby, it's fantastic," he said. His gray eyes crinkled down at her in his special smile.

"Yeah," Shelby said.

"You deserve to go too," he said. "You're the best, Shel. The very best."

"Aw, you're prejudiced." Shelby's eyes slid away from his. "I wish. . .you're just as good as Jude Jefferson, or Murph or Pete. Or little Blinky Martinez."

"No I'm not." Brian ran the flat of his hand along his skateboard wheels, making them spin and whirr. Cadillac wheels, Chicago trucks, the whole machine crafted for speed. But his speed on the slalom tryouts wasn't fast enough. He'd placed fourth, and they'd just picked two speed skaters. The first two.

Now other kids were swarming around them, all trying to congratulate Shelby at once.

"Some people have all the luck," someone said. "Four weeks away. And getting to go to all those neat places."

Ding Dong, their manager, yelled to make himself heard.

"Listen, it's going to be fun, OK. But if you skaters think that's all it's going to be you're crazy. We'll be driving for hours between shows and competitions. It'll be hard work, and bed every night by nine. Elena and I are going to be stricter than your own parents, right Elena?"

Elena nodded. She was Mrs. Bell, Ding Dong's wife, and Shelby couldn't imagine her being strict about anything.

A voice spoke behind them. "Sorry you didn't make it, Brian."

Shelby turned. It was Jude Jefferson.

Why didn't you just stay away, Shelby thought. Standing there, gloating, all pleased with yourself. She had a hard time admitting to herself that Jude didn't really look that way at all. As a matter of fact he looked uncomfortable, as if he'd pulled off something sneaky.

Which of course he hadn't. He was good. Real good.

"That's the way it goes," Brian said and turned away.

Shelby saw Jude shrug and raise his eyebrows. Well, what did he expect from Brian? Brian was disappointed.

"Pain!" Shelby muttered.

Little Cathy Martin wriggled her way through to them. Her face was so red it almost matched her hair. "Oh, wow, Shelby," she said. The words came out, fast and abrupt as a hiccup.

Shelby laughed. "Take it easy, Cath. You'll have a heart attack before the tour even begins."

Cathy took a deep breath. "I didn't think I'd make it. I'm not great looking on a board the way you are."

"Yes you are," Shelby said. "We do different things, is all."

"Hey, can we be roommates? Elena says mostly we'll be sharing in twos."

"Sure," Shelby said.

"And sit together in the bus?"

"That too."

Cathy's face simmered down a little. Shelby figured she was probably a bit scared as well as excited. Cathy was only thirteen. She'd be the youngest of the eight going on the trip. But young or not, she was a good choice. Cathy could make a skateboard do just about anything and judges always fell for her smallness and the perkiness of her carroty braids.

"You know, I think we've got a pretty strong team," she told Brian as they walked

home. "Cath and Linda for the trick skating, Deb for the slalom and me for freestyle." She didn't mention the four boys in case it would hurt Brian's feelings. He didn't mention them either. Not then. But on the night before the tour began he did.

They stood on Shelby's porch, lingering over their goodnights. Shelby buried her face in his throat, smelling the skin smell of him that she knew so well. The top button of his shirt was hard against her face.

"It's going to be a long summer," he muttered into her hair. Then he said, "I wouldn't mind you going so much if Jude Jefferson wasn't going too."

"What?" Shelby pulled back, trying to see him in the glimmer of light that filtered through from the hallway.

"He likes you," Brian said.

Shelby stared at the blur of his face. "Are you kidding? He can't stand me. And I feel the same about him. Just today he was trying to tell me to point my toe more in my Royal Christie. What does he know? Ding Dong says I do it just right. I told Jude to concentrate on doing his stuff and let me do mine."

"He likes you," Brian said again. "And you're going to be with him for just about every minute for the next four weeks."

"Oh, Brian!" Shelby stood on tiptoe and brushed a light kiss across his cheek. "You don't have to worry. Four weeks will go so fast! I won't pay any attention to Jude Jefferson or anyone else. I'm your girl, for always." They were words she'd said to him before and meant with all her heart.

Brian held her then and his kiss wasn't light and gentle. There was a fierceness in it that she wasn't ready for and couldn't handle. "See you soon," she whispered, pulling away.

In bed, she lay looking at the shadowy shapes of her duffle bag and sleeping bag. Her two skateboards waited on her dresser. Her jeans and the yellow sweat shirt that said Wayne Skateboards on it in big black letters were laid out over a chair.

There was a little tap at her door and her mom poked her head around. "You going to be able to sleep, honey?" she whispered.

"I sure am," Shelby whispered back.

"Well, see you in the morning."

But it wasn't as easy to sleep as she'd thought it would be. And no matter how she tried to reassure Brian, four weeks was a long time.

He didn't come to Ding Dong's house in the morning to say goodbye. Shelby was glad. They'd said their goodbyes last night.

Her dad had a last few words with Ding Dong. Shelby noticed that most of the other parents did too.

Ding Dong looked very stern and fatherly, and Elena wasn't wearing her usual cut off jeans and tatty T-shirt. They both looked stable and adult and trustworthy, and all the parents smiled at each other, relieved.

"There's something for you in your duffle bag, Shelby," her dad said. "Brian came over this morning before you came downstairs. He asked me to put it with your things. You're to open it on the way."

"What is it?"

"A little package. I put it down the side. He says it isn't breakable."

"Oh." Shelby felt like crying. And up to now she'd been doing real well.

"Everyone aboard," Ding-Dong yelled. "First stop San Francisco." Shelby hugged her mom and dad and climbed on the mini-bus. "Bye," she whispered.

She stared out of the window and saw Jude Jefferson saying goodbye to his parents and little brother. The sun turned his hair almost silver. When he speed skated he wore an Indian band around it to keep it out of his eyes. He always leaned way over on his board, sort of folding the length of him across it. Funny, how

graceful he was on a board. He was always kind of gangly looking off it.

"All aboard, I said," Ding Dong yelled and Jude tousled his little brother's hair and swung on the mini-bus.

Shelby turned her face away. She'd never really thought much about Jude before and she knew she was thinking about him now because of what Brian had said. She waved out of the window at her mom and dad. Honestly, she thought, just because Brian likes me he thinks every other guy does too. But I wish he hadn't said that to me anyway, about Jude. I just wish he hadn't.

The bus was pulling away now and they were all waving, shouting last goodbyes. Cath was snuffling as she came to sit beside Shelby.

"It's OK, Cath," Shelby said. She unpeeled a stick of gum and gave Cathy half.

"It's so dumb," Cathy whispered. "I'm really happy, you know, that they picked me. It's just. . ."

"I know."

Everyone was kind of quiet at first, but after a bit they loosened up. By the time they were out on the Ventura Freeway, moving along with the traffic, they'd begun to sing and horse around. Ding Dong conducted with one finger till Elena told him to keep both hands on the wheel.

Shelby got up and went between the seats to the back of the bus where the luggage was piled. Her blue duffel bag, of course, was almost on the bottom. She got a grip on one of its loops and tugged.

"Need some help?"

Jude was turned round in his seat, watching her.

"It's OK," Shelby said. But she found she couldn't budge the bag unless she moved everything else off the top. She started lifting away back packs and sleeping bags.

"Here." Jude slung a couple of suitcases out of the way. "The blue one's yours, isn't it?"

"Yes." Shelby pushed her hair back and smiled up at him. Why did Brian think he liked her anyway? Had somebody told him?

"Thanks," she said and waited till he was back in his seat before she unzipped the bag. She pushed her hand down the side and right away found the box.

It was covered with Christmas paper. A bedraggled red bow was stuck on top.

Shelby smiled and felt a rush of tenderness. Wasn't that just like Brian? He'd think nothing of Christmas paper in July. Gift wrap was gift wrap.

She put the duffle bag back and carried the box to her seat.

For always

"What is it?" Cathy asked.

"I don't know. It's from Brian." Shelby unstuck the tape and pulled off the paper. Inside was a small white box. She lifted the lid and took out the thin silver chain that glinted in the sunlight. There was a disc hanging from it. Shelby held it up. The words Brian and Shelby were printed on it. Inside it said, "For always."

She blinked and knew that she couldn't see to open the clasp. She held the bracelet out to Cathy. "Look! Isn't it gorgeous?"

Cathy's eyes opened wide. "How pretty!" She bent forward to read the words. "He really likes you, Shelby, huh? I wonder if anybody will ever like me that way?"

Shelby swallowed and smiled. "Sure. Blinky Gonzales does already. Haven't you noticed the way he stares at you?" Blinky was fourteen.

Cathy smoothed her braids. "Honest?"

Shelby opened the catch and put the little chain around her wrist. "For always" she thought. That's the way it is for Brian and me.

They drove all morning stopping to eat a late lunch in San Luis Obispo. Ding Dong knew a park that had shade trees and picnic tables. It also had swings.

Shelby pushed Cathy and then she got on while Cathy pushed her.

"I'm too big for this," she shrieked, loving every second of the hot wind blowing her hair, the sky rushing down to meet her. She wondered where little Cathy got the strength to push her so hard and then discovered that someone else had taken over, and it was Jude pushing now, his hands strong and hard on her shoulders.

"I've had enough," she yelled and he let her die down, catching the chains to pull her around toward him as the swing stopped.

His face was very close to hers. His eyes

had little darker flecks in them and the lashes were dark brown, much browner than his hair.

Something strange was happening to her stomach.

"I. . .I haven't been on a swing for so long," she stammered, and he took his hands from the chains so she could brush past him and walk away.

Cathy napped away the afternoon miles, her head heavy against Shelby's shoulder. Shelby stared at the Northern California hills rolling on either side of the freeway and she wished and wished that Brian had made the team too. It wasn't going to be any fun without him.

But it was fun. They took part in their first contest the day after they arrived in San Francisco. It was in the Cow Palace which was a nice old building in spite of its weird name.

There were about eleven teams entered for the contest.

"You see that guy?" Jude asked her at warm ups, pointing to a small boy of about fourteen with straight, black hair. "That's Jonny Ho, a real hot-dog speed skater from Hawaii. Caliber Skateboards brings him over specially to wear its colors in its contests."

"I bet he isn't any faster than you," Shelby said. "Or Pete," she added. For some reason

she felt guilty at her quick reaction to Jude's competition. What did she care if the Hawaiian champion beat him? Except that it would lose points for the whole Wayne Skateboard team. Team loyalty was a pretty strong thing.

Basic loyalty, she told herself again as she stood on the sidelines watching the competitors line up for the start of the slalom.

The event organizers had done a real good job of setting up the Cow Palace.

The freestyle arena where she'd perform next was wide and smooth, ringed with seats. And the ramps for the slalom were nicely graded, the lanes clearly marked with white paint. An attendant had just set up the last of the red and white cones.

Cathy and Shelby stood together.

"Come on, Pete. Come on Jude," Cathy yelled. She drank orange juice from a paper cup. Lucky her, Shelby thought. Her event's over and she can relax. Especially since she took a good second. "I wonder why the freestyle's always last," she grumbled.

"Because it's the prettiest," Cathy said. "Hey, they're starting."

The announcer read off the names and the teams they represented. Jude was probably the tallest guy in the event. He and Pete wore their yellow Wayne T-shirts and shorts. A red

sweat band held back Jude's light hair. The Hawaiian had drawn a good spot by the rail.

The starting gun popped.

Jude pushed off strongly, picking up speed as he came to the first gate.

"Go, Jude! Go!" Shelby's nails cut into the palms of her hands. He and Jonny Ho were neck and neck.

The roar of the crowd grew as the skateboarders caromed up the second ramp and down the grade to the homestretch.

"Pete's going to get third," Cathy yelled and Shelby shifted her eyes from the brown and yellow crouched figure on the blue skateboard to Pete and knew instantly that her whole mind had been zeroed in on Jude.

"And Jude, Jude's going to beat the other guy, he's going to. Come on, Jude!" Cathy yelled.

He'd pulled a first. Shelby could hardly believe it. She'd known he was good, but not that good.

The announcer's voice called off the standings.

"Jude Jefferson of Wayne Skateboards, first.

"Jonny Ho, Caliber Skateboards, second.

"Pete Rogers, also Wayne Skateboards, third."

Ding Dong had run out to pump Jude's hand and thump Pete on the back. Cathy had dashed out too. Shelby hung back.

Jude looked across at her and she wondered how he'd known so accurately where she was. Had he known all the time? All the time he was skating?

"Terrific," she told him. "Great job, Pete."

"Your turn, Shelby girl," Ding Dong said. "Better get on over to the freestyle arena."

"Yeah really." Her hands were sweaty on her skateboard and she shifted it under her other arm.

"You don't have a thing to worry about, Shel," Cathy said, "You're way cuter than all those other girls."

"And better too," Jude said. "Just keep that toe pointed."

Shelby gave him a frustrated look and joined the free skaters, warming up.

She and Ding Dong had worked for hours and hours putting together her routine. She skated to the theme from "Love Story," every move planned to match the music, the graceful rise and fall of the melody. She was Number 3, skating third.

The two girls ahead of her were good. The judges scored them 7s and 8s. Shelby felt unsure of herself, nervous, as the first notes of "Love Story" swelled into the arena.

But when she got started it was the way it always was. The muted purr of her skateboard wheels on asphalt, the way the board responded to every move of her body, the two of them, together, a team.

Rolling forward, stretching her arms gracefully in front and lifting one leg behind she heard the applause begin, like the low swell of the sea, as she came into her Arabesque.

Moving out of that, crouching for her Royal Christie that stretched her left leg to one side and her arms to the other she heard the sighs and little rustlings that meant the audience held its breath, spellbound. Point the toe, she thought suddenly and she knew exactly where Jude stood by the railing, knew without looking. See, she told him wordlessly. I'm doing what you told me.

The record was slowing to an end. She went into her finale, the spinner, that made her hair fly around her like a veil as she jumped from the board to spin back on to it again. She did her back lift then, flipping the board from the ground into her waiting hands, and bowed.

"Oh wow," Cathy said. "You were fantastic, Shel."

"Was I OK?" she asked Ding Dong, pushing back her tangled hair.

"Kid, you were better than OK." Ding Dong spoke in a hushed voice, as if they were in church.

The judges must have thought she was OK too.

"Look at that," Jude said. "Three nines and two perfect tens."

"I tell you," Ding Dong said, "we have got us some team."

There was no denying it. At the end of the meet they had enough points to take an over all first.

When they got back to the motel Ding Dong rushed to the phone to call Mr. Wayne, the skateboard manufacturer who was sponsoring the tour. When he came back he said, "Mr. Wayne says congratulations, and steaks for everybody."

"It's good promotion for his boards," Murph said.

"So?" Shelby asked. "They're good boards. We ought to know."

Ding Dong said he'd heard about a place in Sausalito where the steaks were great and not too expensive. And there was a view of the bay.

Shelby and Cathy decided to get all stepped up. They shook out the only dresses they'd brought and hung them in the bathroom while they took their showers.

"Do you think my legs will grow as long as yours?" Cathy asked holding out one of her stubby, red fuzzed ones. "I heard one of those girls you beat today saying its only because of your long legs that you won. Because they look so good in ballet. I guess I'm going to have, to stick with wheelies and daffies and handstands unless my legs grow."

"You want to know a secret?" Shelby asked. "I can't do a handstand. Not on the board and not off either."

"No kidding?" Cathy beamed. "I guess we're all good at different things." She watched Shelby zippering the back of her white sleeveless dress. "But you're so gorgeous. I wouldn't mind not being able to do handstands if I looked like you."

Shelby laughed. She'd taken off her bracelet while she showered and now she fastened it back on. The little silver disc winked up at her. For always. How could she be so happy when Brian wasn't here? She decided she'd call him before they left. But there wasn't time.

"We have 7:30 reservations," Ding Dong said. He shooed them in front of him like a flock of geese. "Get in the bus."

Shelby didn't know how it happened.

Pete grabbed Cathy as she was passing and said, "Hey Shrimp, sit with me. I can't figure how you do that headstand without scraping the skin off your face."

And suddenly, unexpectedly, Jude had slipped into the empty seat beside Shelby.

They didn't talk at all. He was wearing beige corduroys and a brown and white striped shirt. His shoulder brushed hers, and once, when

Ding Dong stopped fast for a red light they bumped against each other.

"Sorry," Shelby said quickly, pulling away.

"Yeah, sorry." A little pink moved up under the tan of his throat.

Shelby turned the silver chain round and around on her wrist and stared out of the window at the cable cars bulging with people and the San Francisco hills that rose and fell in front of them like the nerve blowers on a switchback railway.

Then they were on the Golden Gate Bridge, driving across the incredible shadowed blues of the bay toward the rolling green hills of Marin County.

"It's unbelievable, isn't it," Shelby whispered, and she meant the night outside, the companionship on the bus, the whole excitement of the day.

They ate at little tables crowded together on a deck that faced the lights of San Francisco. Small sailboats drifted around Alcatraz Island, spreading their sails in search of a wind that wasn't there.

There was a jukebox inside and a small dance floor.

Ding Dong chuckled. He borrowed a quarter from Elena and fed it to the machine.

It was an old Beatle record that he'd chosen. "Hey Jude."

"C'mon, Jude, dance with me," Cathy said, but Pete grabbed her and pulled her into some weird dance that he said was called the funky squirrel and that he'd invented.

And Shelby was dancing with Jude, his hands warm on her shoulders, dancing close, the old-fashioned way. Early moonlight slanted through the open windows and there was the far away whisper of the bay washing the beach.

Again they didn't talk. There was a sort of electricity that seemed to flow between them and Shelby was terribly aware of his arm, so close to her face, the silver hairs glinting against its brownness, his fingers with their squared off nails.

The whole team and Ding Dong and Elena went for a walk on the little beach before they went back to the motel. Shelby made sure she stayed between Ding Dong and Elena. This strange new awareness of Jude was bothering her. And she made sure she sat next to little Cathy on the bus going back.

"You know what?" Cathy said. "I think Pete was just keeping me busy so Jude could get to be with you. I think Jude fixed it that way."

"Oh, don't be silly," Shelby said. "Why should he do that?"

She slept that night with Brian's chain under her pillow. "Oh, Brian," she whispered. "And this is only the end of the second day. Twenty-six more to go."

The next day they drove up Interstate 5 into Oregon and gave an exhibition on that Saturday in Portland. By the middle of the second week they were in Seattle, facing another competition.

Shelby had written three postcards to Brian. Twice she'd called him. But on one of those times he hadn't been home. She felt very far away from him and each day he seemed to recede more and more into the past. More and more life was bounded by those in the team. They had their own jokes now and there was a growing and special closeness between them. Shelby noticed that Cathy was spending a lot of time with Blinky Martinez. Once she found a crumpled piece of paper on the dresser where Cathy had written Cathy Martinez ten times and Mrs. Blinky Martinez ten more. There was also a very fancy heart with I LOVE BLINKY printed in it.

Shelby herself alternated between days of despair and guilt and days of perfect happiness. There had been some special moments in Seattle that she couldn't keep out of her mind.

Ding Dong had taken the team to the top of the Space Needle for lunch. They wore their

Wayne T shirts. "Mr. Wayne's paying for all the advertising we can give him," Ding Dong said.

From the Needle the waters of the Sound looked like frozen silk. A speed boat left a trail of white, wispy as smoke.

Shelby looked down and felt the dizziness come. Heights had always bothered her, but this time she held on to the railing, and felt her knees crumple.

"Shel, hold on to me. It's all right." Jude's arm was around her and she felt herself slump against him as he led her back, away from the terrible space that gaped below.

They sat inside on a bench by the concession stand and Shelby was shivering and shaking as if she'd never stop.

"Sh, sh, honey. You're safe. You're OK." He smoothed her hair away from her face and she felt his lips on her cheek and he was holding her and whispering things to her, things she couldn't hear, didn't want to hear.

Ding Dong came then and brought her coffee and it was over. Except that she couldn't forget it.

"Do you like Jude?" Cathy whispered one night as they lay in the dark of their motel room. They were turned around now, heading back through Idaho to California. By every standard the tour had been a success. They'd placed first and second constantly. They'd had

television coverage and newspaper coverage, and one guy was riding the bus with them now, making a real Skateboard movie. Mr. Wayne had had more publicity for his skateboards than even he could have hoped for.

"Well do you?" Cathy persisted.

"I like everybody."

"Oh rats, Shelby. You know what I mean. The way I like Blinky."

"Don't be silly. I'm Brian's girl," Shelby said. The words didn't have their usual sureness and for the first time she didn't add the extra special ones, for always.

"Ha, ha," Cathy said and didn't answer when Shelby asked her "What's ha-ha supposed to mean?"

It was in Reno, Nevada, that Cathy lost Blinky. She caught him holding hands with a little, blonde skateboarder on the Reno Astroboards team.

"And she was so cute, Shelby," Cathy sobbed. "She had blonde bangs. She looked just like a mouseketeer."

Shelby tried not to laugh. She knew how awful Cathy felt. But it was hard to stay serious when Cathy said, "We were planning on getting engaged in three years. When I'm sixteen."

"The little blonde will have to stay here,"

Shelby comforted her. "You'll see. When we move on, you'll get Blinky back."

"I don't want him back. He told me he'd love me forever. Forever! And then he went off with the first little cute Mouseketeer he met."

"Cathy, honey. It's dumb to talk about forever at thirteen. The world's full of guys. You'll meet a hundred you like before you're sixteen and a hundred more after that."

She heard her own words and something about them made her stand up quickly and move to the window to stare out at the brown Nevada lawn and the lighted square of the pool. There was no forever when you were thirteen. And no for always when you were sixteen either. Life stretched ahead, full of adventure and excitement.

She touched the silver chain of her bracelet and she loved it, knowing that she had been resenting it for days. Resenting it because of the guilt she felt each time she looked at it.

Oh, Brian, I'll be back, she thought. But for now, I'm here, and next year, who knows where I'll be. Or you either. We have all the time in the world to decide if we want what we have to be forever. We don't need to decide at sixteen.

Someone thumped on the door.

"Hey you guys," Pete yelled. "We're all going swimming."

"Cathy," Shelby said, "it's not the end of the world. Honest. Come on, let's jump in the pool. You know what swimming does? It makes your legs grow longer."

She searched the blue duffel bag for her swimsuit. Everyone would be out there. Jude too, and that was OK. Her heart seemed to suddenly skip a beat and she knew there was a breathlessness, a bubbling inside her just at the thought of seeing him again.

But that was OK. That was OK too.